INTERNATIONAL POCKET LIBRARY
EDITED BY EDMUND R. BROWN

T5-AEX-060

TWO WESSEX TALES

TWO WESSEX TALES

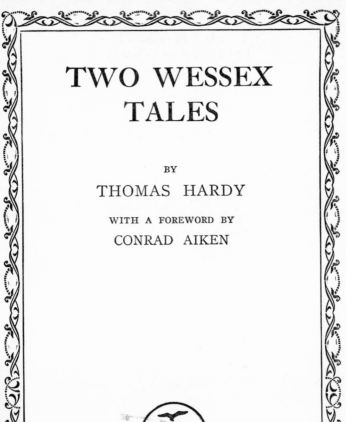

BY

THOMAS HARDY

WITH A FOREWORD BY

CONRAD AIKEN

BOSTON

INTERNATIONAL POCKET LIBRARY

THOMAS HARDY

THOMAS HARDY and George Meredith have often been coupled as the last of the Victorians. In both cases the term,—as journalistic terms are too apt to be,— is peculiarly inappropriate. Neither Meredith nor Hardy is Victorian, except in the sense that they began their careers before the end of that period. Rightly or wrongly, a certain smug righteousness, professional optimism, a determined brightness of outlook, are generally associated with the art which the Victorian era has bequeathed to us. Even Browning and Arnold, in some respects the finest minds of the time, did not altogether escape this. It was left to Meredith and Hardy to break the tradition.

Perhaps it would be more precise to say that the Victorians found it always necessary to lean upon something. Darwin had, for the acuter minds of his generation, shaken religion to its foundations; and there was in consequence a somewhat frantic hurry to find, among those foundations, fragments solid enough to lean upon, and abstract enough to remain untouched by the doctrine of evolution. Can the earth-philosophy which Meredith turned towards be called one of these fragments? He found some such emotional and ethical substitute necessary, at any rate. It was Hardy who first walked forth without light into the wilderness.

Hardy is a novelist, in consequence, who supremely

demands that his reader shall have courage. He offers no bright panaceas, no subtle consolations. He is a merciless determinist, a passionate ironist. He sees the life of man as a harsh glare of prearranged tragedy, and he takes pleasure in standing, helpless but resolute, in the full dreadfulness of this glare. It has been said that Hardy is cruel to his characters, that he persecutes them, that he delights in whipping them from disaster to disaster. This is both true and false: true, in the sense that, as an artist, Hardy takes the keenest of all pleasures in getting at the essentials of man's nature, in showing him to be forever the victim of his own divergent instincts, drawn this way and that, setting up for himself lofty ideals only to fail of attainment, alternately wise and foolish, ugly and beautiful; false, in the sense that it assumes Hardy to be a sort of monster of indifference,—whereas in fact he is the profoundest of humanists. For it is not man he indicts, in the end, but the fates, the chances, the mechanical shuffle of forces which have made man the blind and blundering creature that he is. "Is it possible that a God would do so cruel a thing?" Hardy asks. "Is there a God at all? If so, then in point of intelligence and generosity man is a long way in advance of him."

In method, Hardy might be called a poetic realist: a term which suggests clearly, as in this case it should, the epic. The best of his novels are, indeed, epics in prose: *Jude the Obscure,* for example. This has an architectural quality, is at the same time as colossal and as beautifully designed as a great cathedral. The prose style used is simple and inconspicuous, a transparent and easy medium. It does not exist for itself, as might be said, for example, of the style of George Moore.

Only rarely does it take on a glow or speed all of its own. But it is supremely adequate to its purpose, an instrument tried and perfected.

The two stories in the present volume are early work, but none the less very typical. If one has a criticism of them it is that the determinism is as yet a little raw, has almost the semblance of melodrama: coincidence is a trifle overstrained. Hardy had not yet acquired the artistic mastery necessary to the concealment of his purpose. He shows us the skeleton a little too clearly. The bones of it protrude too frequently. And in consequence one does not surrender to the thesis as willingly as one does in the later work,—in which, indeed, one does not surrender, one is, rather, simply mastered. Nevertheless, these two stories contain in germ all that we have come to associate with Hardy. The determinism is present; the preoccupation with rural rather than with urban men and scenes; the vigorous and unswerving march of the narrative.

CONRAD AIKEN

TWO WESSEX TALES

THE THREE STRANGERS

AMONG the few features of agricultural England which retain an appearance but little modified by the lapse of centuries, may be reckoned the high, grassy, and furzy downs, coombs, or ewe-leases, as they are indifferently called, that fill a large area of certain counties in the south and south-west. If any mark of human occupation is met with hereon it usually takes the form of the solitary cottage of some shepherd.

Fifty years ago such a lonely cottage stood on such a down, and may possibly be standing there now. In spite of its loneliness, however, the spot, by actual measurement, was not more than five miles from a county-town. Yet that affected it little. Five miles of irregular upland, during the long inimical seasons, with their sleets, snows, rains, and mists, afford withdrawing space enough to isolate a Timon or a Nebuchadnezzar; much less, in fair weather, to please that less repellent tribe, the poets, philosophers, artists, and others who "conceive and meditate of pleasing things."

Some old earthen camp or barrow, some clump of trees, at least some starved fragment of ancient hedge, is usually taken advantage of in the erection of these forlorn dwellings. But, in the present case, such a kind of shelter had been disregarded. Higher Crowstairs, as the house was called, stood quite detached and undefended. The only reason for its precise situation seemed to be the crossing of two foot-paths at right angles hard by, which may have crossed there and thus for a good five hundred years. Hence the house was exposed to the elements on all sides. But, though the wind up here blew unmistakably when it did blow, and the rain hit hard whenever it fell, the various weathers of the winter season were not quite so formidable on the coomb as they were imagined to be by dwellers on low ground. The raw rimes were not so pernicious as in the hollows, and the frosts were scarcely so severe. When the shepherd and his family who tenanted the house were pitied for their sufferings from the exposure, they said that upon the whole they were less inconvenienced by "wuzzes and flames" (hoarses and phlegms) than when they had lived by the stream of a snug neighboring valley.

The night of March 28, 182—, was precisely one of the nights that were wont to call forth these expressions of commiseration. The level rain-storm smote walls, slopes, and hedges like the clothyard shafts of Senlac and Crécy. Such sheep and out-door animals as had no shelter stood with their buttocks to the wind; while the tails of little birds trying to roost on some scraggy thorn were blown inside out like umbrellas. The gable end of the cottage was stained with wet, and the eavesdropping flapped against the wall. Yet never was commiseration for the shepherd more misplaced, for that cheerful rustic was entertaining a large party in glorification of the christening of his second girl.

The guests had arrived before the rain began to fall, and they were all now assembled in the chief, or living, room of the dwelling. A glance into the apartment at

eight o'clock on this eventful evening would have re-
sulted in the opinion that it was as cosey and comfortable a nook as could be wished for in boisterous
weather. The calling of its inhabitant was proclaimed
by a number of highly polished sheep-crooks without
stems that were hung ornamentally over the fireplace,
the curl of each shining crook varying from the anti-
quated type engraved in the patriarchal pictures of old
family Bibles to the most approved fashion of the last
local sheep-fair. The room was lighted by half a dozen
candles, having wicks only a trifle smaller than the
grease which enveloped them, in candlesticks that were
never used but at high-days, holy-days, and family
feasts. The lights were scattered about the room, two
of them standing on the chimney-piece. This position
of candles was in itself significant. Candles on the
chimney-piece always meant a party.

On the hearth, in front of a back-brand to give sub-
stance, blazed a fire of thorns, that crackled "like the
laughter of the fool."

Nineteen persons were gathered here. Of these, five
women, wearing gowns of various bright hues, sat in
chairs along the wall; girls shy and not shy filled the
window-bench; four men, including Charley Jake, the
hedge-carpenter, Elijah New, the parish-clerk, and
John Pitcher, a neighboring dairy-man, the shepherd's
father-in-law, lolled in the settle; a young man and
maid, who were blushing over tentative *pourparlers* on
a life-companionship, sat beneath the corner cupboard;
and an elderly engaged man of fifty or upwards moved
restlessly about from spots where his betrothed was not
to the spot where she was. Enjoyment was pretty general, and so much the more prevailed in being unham-

pered by conventional restrictions. Absolute confidence
in one another's good opinion begot perfect ease, while
the finishing stroke of manner, amounting to a truly
princely serenity, was lent to the majority by the absence of any expression or trait denoting that they
wished to get on in the world, enlarge their minds, or
do any eclipsing thing whatever—which nowadays so
generally nips the bloom and *bonhomie* of all except
the two extremes of the social scale.

Shepherd Fennel had married well, his wife being a
dairy-man's daughter from the valley below, who
brought fifty guineas in her pocket—and kept them
there till they should be required for ministering to the
needs of a coming family. This frugal woman had
been somewhat exercised as to the character that should
be given to the gathering. A sit-still party had its ad-
vantages; but an undisturbed position of ease in chairs
and settles was apt to lead on the men to such an un-
conscionable deal of toping that they would sometimes
fairly drink the house dry. A dancing-party was the al-
ternative; but this, while avoiding the foregoing objec-
tion on the score of good drink, had a counterbalancing
disadvantage in the matter of good victuals, the raven-
ous appetites engendered by the exercise causing immense havoc in the buttery. Shepherdess Fennel fell
back upon the intermediate plan of mingling short
dances with short periods of talk and singing, so as to
hinder any ungovernable rage in either. But this
scheme was entirely confined to her own gentle mind;
the shepherd himself was in the mood to exhibit the
most reckless phases of hospitality.

The fiddler was a boy of those parts, about twelve
years of age, who had a wonderful dexterity in jigs

and reels, though his fingers were so small and short as to necessitate a constant shifting for the high notes, from which he scrambled back to the first position with sounds not of unmixed purity of tone. At seven the shrill tweedle-dee of this youngster had begun, accompanied by a booming ground-bass from Elijah New, the parish-clerk, who had thoughtfully brought with him his favorite musical instrument, the serpent. Dancing was instantaneous, Mrs. Fennel privately enjoining the players on no account to let the dance exceed the length of a quarter of an hour.

But Elijah and the boy, in the excitement of their position, quite forgot the injunction. Moreover, Oliver Giles, a man of seventeen, one of the dancers, who was enamoured of his partner, a fair girl of thirty-three rolling years, had recklessly handed a new crown-piece to the musicians, as a bribe to keep going as long as they had muscle and wind. Mrs. Fennel, seeing the steam begin to generate on the countenances of her guests, crossed over and touched the fiddler's elbow and put her hand on the serpent's mouth. But they took no notice, and fearing she might lose her character of genial hostess if she were to interfere too markedly, she retired and sat down helplessly. And so the dance whizzed on with cumulative fury, the performers moving in their planet-like courses, direct and retrograde, from apogee to perigee, till the hand of the well-kicked clock at the bottom of the room had travelled over the circumference of an hour.

While these cheerful events were in course of enactment within Fennel's pastoral dwelling, an incident having considerable bearing on the party had occurred in the gloomy night without. Mrs. Fennel's concern about the growing fierceness of the dance corresponded in point of time with the ascent of a human figure to the solitary hill of Higher Crowstairs from the direction of the distant town. This personage strode on through the rain without a pause, following the little-worn path which, farther on in its course, skirted the shepherd's cottage.

It was nearly the time of full moon, and on this account, though the sky was lined with a uniform sheet of dripping cloud, ordinary objects out-of-doors were readily visible. The sad, wan light revealed the lonely pedestrian to be a man of supple frame; his gait suggested that he had somewhat passed the period of perfect and instinctive agility, though not so far as to be otherwise than rapid of motion when occasion required. In point of fact, he might have been about forty years of age. He appeared tall, but a recruiting sergeant, or other person accustomed to the judging of men's heights by the eye, would have discerned that this was chiefly owing to his gauntness, and that he was not more than five feet eight or nine.

Notwithstanding the regularity of his tread there was caution in it, as in that of one who mentally feels his way; and despite the fact that it was not a black coat nor a dark garment of any sort that he wore, there was something about him which suggested that he naturally belonged to the black-coated tribes of men. His clothes were of fustian, and his boots hobnailed, yet in his progress he showed not the mud-accustomed bearing of hobnailed and fustianed peasantry.

By the time that he had arrived abreast of the shepherd's premises the rain came down, or rather came along, with yet more determined violence. The out-skirts of the little settlement partially broke the force of wind and rain, and this induced him to stand still. The most salient of the shepherd's domestic erections was an empty sty at the forward corner of his hedgeless garden, for in these latitudes the principle of masking the homelier features of your establishment by a conventional frontage was unknown. The traveller's eye was attracted to this small building by the pallid shine of the wet slates that covered it. He turned aside, and, finding it empty, stood under the pent-roof for shelter.

While he stood, the boom of the serpent within the adjacent house, and the lesser strains of the fiddler, reached the spot as an accompaniment to the surging hiss of the flying rain on the sod, its louder beating on the cabbage-leaves of the garden, on the eight or ten beehives just discernible by the path, and its dripping from the eaves into a row of buckets and pans that had been placed under the walls of the cottage. For at Higher Crowstairs, as at all such elevated domiciles, the grand difficulty of house-keeping was an insufficiency of water; and a casual rainfall was utilized by turning out, as catchers, every utensil that the house contained. Some queer stories might be told of the contrivances for economy in suds and dishwaters that are absolutely necessitated in upland habitations during the droughts of summer. But at this season there were no such exigencies; a mere acceptance of what the skies bestowed was sufficient for an abundant store.

At last the notes of the serpent ceased, and the house was silent. This cessation of activity aroused the solitary pedestrian from the reverie into which he had

lapsed, and, emerging from the shed, with an apparently
new intention, he walked up the path to the house door.
Arrived here, his first act was to kneel down on a large
stone beside the row of vessels, and to drink a copious
draught from one of them. Having quenched his thirst
he rose and lifted his hand to knock, but paused with
his eye upon the panel. Since the dark surface of the
wood revealed absolutely nothing, it was evident that he
must be mentally looking through the door, as if he
wished to measure thereby all the possibilities that a
house of this sort might include, and how they might
bear upon the question of his entry.

In his indecision he turned and surveyed the scene
around. Not a soul was anywhere visible. The garden
path stretched downward from his feet, gleaming like
the track of a snail; the roof of the little well (mostly
dry), the well-cover, the top rail of the garden gate,
were varnished with the same dull liquid glaze; while,
far away in the vale, a faint whiteness of more than
usual extent showed that the rivers were high in the
meads. Beyond all this winked a few bleared lamp-
lights through the beating drops, lights that denoted the
situation of the county-town from which he had appeared to come. The absence of all notes of life in that
direction seemed to clinch his intentions, and he knocked
at the door.

Within, a desultory chat had taken the place of movement and musical sound. The hedge-carpenter was sug-
gesting a song to the company, which nobody just then
was inclined to undertake, so that the knock afforded a
not unwelcome diversion.

"Walk in," said the shepherd, promptly.

The latch clicked upward, and out of the night our pedestrian appeared upon the door-mat. The shepherd arose, snuffed two of the nearest candles, and turned to look at him.

Their light disclosed that the stranger was dark in complexion and not unprepossessing as to feature. His hat, which for a moment he did not remove, hung low over his eyes, without concealing that they were large, open, and determined, moving with a flash rather than a glance round the room. He seemed pleased with the survey, and, baring his shaggy head, said, in a rich deep voice, "The rain is so heavy, friends, that I ask leave to come in and rest a while."

"To be sure, stranger," said the shepherd. "And faith, you've been lucky in choosing your time, for we are having a bit of a fling for a glad cause—though, to be sure, a man could hardly wish that glad cause to happen more than once a year."

"Nor less," spoke up a woman. "For 'tis best to get your family over and done with, as soon as you can, so as to be all the earlier out of the fag o't."

"And what may be this glad cause?" asked the stranger.

"A birth and christening," said the shepherd.

The stranger hoped his host might not be made unhappy either by too many or too few of such episodes, and being invited by a gesture to a pull at the mug, he readily acquiesced. His manner, which, before entering, had been so dubious, was now altogether that of a careless and candid man.

"Late to be traipsing athwart this coomb—hey?" said the engaged man of fifty.

"Late it is, master, as you say. I'll take a seat in the chimney-corner, if you have nothing to urge against it, ma'am, for I am a little moist on the side that was next the rain."

Mrs. Shepherd Fennel assented, and made room for the self-invited comer, who having got completely inside the chimney-corner, stretched out his legs and his arms with the expansiveness of a person quite at home.

"Yes, I am rather thin in the vamp," he said, freely, seeing that the eye of the shepherd's wife fell upon his boots, "and I am not well fitted, either. I have had some rough times lately, and have been forced to pick up what I can get in the way of wearing, but I must find a suit better fit for working-days when I reach home."

"One of hereabouts?" she inquired.

"Not quite that—farther up the country."

"I thought so. And so am I; and by your tongue you come from my neighborhood."

"But you would hardly have heard of me," he said quickly. "My time would be long before yours, ma'am, you see."

This testimony to the youthfulness of his hostess had the effect of stopping her cross-examination.

"There is only one thing more wanted to make me happy," continued the newcomer, "and that is a little baccy, which I am sorry to say I am out of."

"I'll fill your pipe," said the shepherd.

"I must ask you to lend me a pipe likewise."

"A smoker, and no pipe about ye?"

"I have dropped it somewhere on the road."

The shepherd filled and handed him a new clay pipe, saying, as he did so, "Hand me your baccy-box—I'll fill that too, now I am about it."

The man went through the movement of searching his pockets.

"Lost that too?" said his entertainer, with some surprise.

"I am afraid so," said the man, with some confusion. "Give it to me in a screw of paper." Lighting his pipe at the candle with a suction that drew the whole flame into the bowl, he resettled himself in the corner, and bent his looks upon the faint steam from his damp leg, as if he wished to say no more.

Meanwhile the general body of guests had been taking little notice of this visitor by reason of an absorbing discussion in which they were engaged with the band about a tune for the next dance. The matter being settled, they were about to stand up, when an interruption came in the shape of another knock at the door.

At sound of the same the man in the chimney-corner took up the poker and began stirring the fire as if doing it thoroughly were the one aim of his existence; and a second time the shepherd said "Walk in!" In a moment another man stood upon the straw-woven door-mat. He, too, was a stranger.

This individual was one of a type radically different from the first. There was more of the commonplace in his manner, and a certain jovial cosmopolitanism sat upon his features. He was several years older than the first arrival, his hair being slightly frosted, his eyebrows bristly, and his whiskers cut back from his cheeks. His face was rather full and flabby, and yet it was not altogether a face without power. A few grog-blossoms marked the neighborhood of his nose. He flung back his long drab great-coat, revealing that beneath it he wore a suit of cinder-gray shade throughout; large, heavy seals

of some metal or other that would take a polish, dang-
ling from his fob, as his only personal ornament. Shaking the water-drops from his low-crowned glazed hat,
he said, "I must ask for a few minutes' shelter, com-
rades, or I shall be wetted to my skin before I get to
Casterbridge."

"Make yourself at home, master," said the shepherd,
perhaps a trifle less heartily than on the first occasion.
Not that Fennel had the least tinge of niggardliness in
his composition; but the room was far from large, spare
chairs were not numerous, and damp companions were
not altogether desirable at close quarters for the women
and girls in their bright-colored gowns.

However, the second comer, after taking off his great-
coat, and hanging his hat on a nail in one of the ceiling-
beams as if he had been specially invited to put it there,
advanced and sat down at the table. This had been
pushed so closely into the chimney-corner, to give all
available room to the dancers, that its inner edge grazed
the elbow of the man who had ensconced himself by the
fire; and thus the two strangers were brought into close
companionship. They nodded to each other by way of
breaking the ice of unacquaintance, and the first stranger handed his neighbor the family mug—a huge vessel
of brown ware, having its upper edge worn away like a
threshold by the rub of whole generations of thirsty lips
that had gone the way of all flesh, and bearing the following inscription burned upon its rotund side in yellow
letters:

THERE iS NO FUN
UNTiL i CUM

The other man, nothing loath, raised the mug to his lips,
and drank on, and on, and on—till a curious blueness

overspread the countenance of the shepherd's wife, who had regarded with no little surprise the first stranger's free offer to the second of what did not belong to him to dispense.

"I knew it!" said the toper to the shepherd, with much satisfaction. "When I walked up your garden before coming in, and saw the hives all of a row I said to myself, 'Where there's bees there's honey, and where there's honey there's mead.' But mead of such a truly comfortable sort as this I really didn't expect to meet in my older days." He took yet another pull at the mug, till it assumed an ominous elevation.

"Glad you enjoy it!" said the shepherd, warmly.

"It is a goodish mead," assented Mrs. Fennel, with an absence of enthusiasm which seemed to say that it was possible to buy praise for one's cellar at too heavy a price. "It is trouble enough to make, and really I hardly think we shall make any more. For honey sells well, and we ourselves can make shift with a drop o' small mead and metheglin for common use from the comb-washings."

"Oh, but you'll never have the heart!" reproachfully cried the stranger in cinder-gray, after taking up the mug a third time and setting it down empty. "I love mead when 'tis old like this, as I love to go to church o' Sundays, or to relieve the needy any day of the week."

"Ha, ha, ha!" said the man in the chimney-corner, who, in spite of the taciturnity induced by the pipe of tobacco, could not or would not refrain from this slight testimony to his comrade's humor.

Now, the old mead of those days, brewed of the purest first-year or maiden honey—four pounds to the

gallon, with its due complement of white of eggs, cin-
namon, ginger, cloves, mace, rosemary, yeast, and pro-
cesses of working, bottling, and cellaring—tasted re-
markably strong; but it did not taste so strong as it
actually was. Hence, presently the stranger in cinder-
gray at the table, moved by its creeping influence, un-
buttoned his waistcoat, threw himself back in his chair,
spread his legs, and made his presence felt in various
ways.

"Well, well, as I say," he resumed, "I am going to
Casterbridge, and to Casterbridge I must go. I should
have been almost there by this time; but the rain drove
me into your dwelling, and I'm not sorry for it."

"You don't live in Casterbridge?" said the shepherd.

"Not as yet, though I shortly mean to move there."

"Going to set up in trade, perhaps?"

"No, no," said the shepherd's wife. "It is easy to see
that the gentleman is rich, and don't want to work at
anything."

The cinder-gray stranger paused, as if to consider
whether he would accept that definition of himself. He
presently rejected it by answering, "Rich is not quite
the word for me, dame. I do work, and I must work.
And even if I only get to Casterbridge by midnight I
must begin work there at eight to-morrow morning.
Yes, het or wet, blow or snow, famine or sword, my
day's work to-morrow must be done."

"Poor man! Then, in spite o' seeming, you be worse
off than we," replied the shepherd's wife.

" 'Tis the nature of my trade, men and maidens. 'Tis
the nature of my trade more than my poverty . . . But
really and truly I must be up and off, or I shan't get a

lodging in the town." However, the speaker did not move, and directly added, "There's time for one more draught of friendship before I go, and I'd perform it at once if the mug were not dry."

"Here's a mug o' small," said Mrs. Fennel. "Small, we call it, though to be sure 'tis only the first wash o' the combs."

"No," said the stranger disdainfully. "I won't spoil your first kindness by partaking o' your second."

"Certainly not," broke in Fennel. "We don't increase and multiply every day, and I'll fill the mug again." He went away to the dark place under the stairs where the barrel stood. The shepherdess followed him.

"Why should you do this?" she said, reproachfully, as soon as they were alone. "He's emptied it once, though it held enough for ten people; and now he's not contented wi' the small, but must needs call for more o' the strong! And a stranger unbeknown to any of us. For my part, I don't like the look o' the man at all."

"But he's in the house, my honey; and 'tis a wet night, and a christening. Daze it, what's a cup of mead or less? there'll be plenty more next bee-burning."

"Very well—this time, then," she answered, looking wistfully at the barrel. "But what is the man's calling, and where is he one of, that he should come in and join us like this?"

"I don't know. I'll ask him again."

The catastrophe of having the mug drained dry at one pull by the stranger in cinder-gray was effectually guarded against this time by Mrs. Fennel. She poured out his allowance in a small cup, keeping the large one at a discreet distance from him. When he had tossed off his portion the shepherd renewed his inquiry about the stranger's occupation.

The latter did not immediately reply, and the man in the chimney-corner, with sudden demonstrativeness, said, "Anybody may know my trade—I'm a wheel-wright."

"A very good trade for these parts," said the shepherd.

"And anybody may know mine—if they've the sense to find it out," said the stranger in cinder-gray.

"You may generally tell what a man is by his claws," observed the hedge-carpenter, looking at his own hands. "My fingers be as full of thorns as an old pincushion is of pins."

The hands of the man in the chimney-corner instinctively sought the shade, and he gazed into the fire as he resumed his pipe. The man at the table took up the hedge-carpenter's remark, and added, smartly, "True; but the oddity of my trade is that, instead of setting a mark upon me it sets a mark upon my customers."

No observation being offered by anybody in elucidation of this enigma, the shepherd's wife once more called for a song. The same obstacles presented themselves as at the former time—one had no voice, another had forgotten the first verse. The stranger at the table, whose soul had now risen to a good working temperature, relieved the difficulty by exclaiming that, to start the company, he would sing himself. Thrusting one thumb into the arm-hole of his waist-coat, he waved the other hand in the air, and, with an extemporizing gaze at the shining sheep-crooks above the mantel-piece, began:

"Oh, my trade it is the rarest one,
            Simple shepherds all—
   My trade is a sight to see;
For my customers I tie, and to take them up on high,
   And waft 'em to a far countree!"

The room was silent when he had finished the verse—
with one exception, that of the man in the chimney-
corner, who, at the singer's word, "Chorus!" joined him
in a deep bass voice of musical relish—

"And waft 'em to a far countree!"

Oliver Giles, John Pitcher the dairy-man, the parish-
clerk, the engaged man of fifty, the row of young wom-
en against the wall, seemed lost in thought not of the
gayest kind. The shepherd looked meditatively on the
ground, the shepherdess gazed keenly at the singer, and
with some suspicion; she was doubting whether this
stranger were merely singing an old song from recol-
lection, or was composing one there and then for the
occasion. All were as perplexed at the obscure revela-
tion as the guests at Belshazzar's Feast, except the man
in the chimney-corner, who quietly said, "Second verse,
stranger," and smoked on.

The singer thoroughly moistened himself from his
lips inward, and went on with the next stanza as re-
quested:

"My tools are but common ones,
            Simple shepherds all—
   My tools are no sight to see;
A little hempen string, and a post whereon to swing,
   Are implements enough for me!"

Shepherd Fennel glanced around. There was no longer any doubt that the stranger was answering his question rhythmically. The guests one and all started back with suppressed exclamations. The young woman engaged to the man of fifty fainted half-way, and would have proceeded, but finding him wanting in alacrity for catching her, she sat down trembling.

"Oh, he's the —— !" whispered the people in the background, mentioning the name of an ominous officer. "He's come to do it. 'Tis to be at Casterbridge jail to-morrow—the man for sheep-stealing—the poor clock-maker we heard of, who used to live away at Shottsford and had no work to do——Timothy Sommers, whose family were a-starving, and so he went out of Shottsford by the high-road, and took a sheep in open daylight, defying the farmer and the farmer's wife and the farmer's lad, and every man jack among 'em. He" (and they nodded towards the stranger of the deadly trade) "is come from up the country to do it because there's not enough to do in his own county-town, and he's got the place here now our own county-man's dead; he's going to live in the same cottage under the prison wall."

The stranger in cinder-gray took no notice of this whispered string of observation, but again wetted his lips. Seeing that his friend in the chimney-corner was the only one who reciprocated his joviality in any way, he held out his cup towards that appreciative comrade, who also held out his own. They clinked together, the eyes of the rest of the room hanging upon the singer's actions. He parted his lips for the third verse, but at that moment another knock was audible upon the door. This time the knock was faint and hesitating.

The company seemed scared; the shepherd looked

with consternation towards the entrance, and it was with some effort that he resisted his alarmed wife's deprecatory glance and uttered for the third time the welcoming words, "Walk in!"

The door was gently opened, and another man stood upon the mat. He, like those who had preceded him, was a stranger. This time it was a short, small personage, of fair complexion, and dressed in a decent suit of dark clothes.

"Can you tell me the way to——?" he began; when, gazing round the room to observe the nature of the company among whom he had fallen, his eyes lighted on the stranger in cinder-gray. It was just at the instant when the latter, who had thrown his mind into his song with such a will that he scarcely heeded the interruption, silenced all whispers and inquiries by bursting into his third verse:

"To-morrow is my working day,
Simple shepherds all—
To-morrow is a working day for me:
For the farmer's sheep is slain, and the lad who did it ta'en,
And on his soul may God ha' merc-y!"

The stranger in the chimney-corner, waving cups with the singer so heartily that his mead splashed over on the hearth, repeated in his bass voice as before:

"And on his soul may God ha' merc-y!"

All this time the third stranger had been standing in the door-way. Finding now that he did not come forward or go on speaking, the guests particularly regarded him. They noticed, to their surprise, that he stood before them the picture of abject terror—his knees trem-

bling, his hand shaking so violently that the door-latch
by which he supported himself rattled audibly; his
white lips were parted, and his eyes fixed on the merry
officer of justice in the middle of the room. A moment
more and he had turned, closed the door, and fled.

"What a man can it be?" said the shepherd.

The rest, between the awfulness of their late discov-
ery and the odd conduct of this third visitor, looked as
if they knew not what to think, and said nothing. Instinctively they withdrew farther and farther from the
grim gentleman in their midst, whom some of them
seemed to take for the Prince of Darkness himself, till
they formed a remote circle, an empty space of floor
being left between them and him—

" . . . circulus, cujus centrum diabolus."

The room was so silent—though there were more than
twenty people in it—that nothing could be heard but the
patter of the rain against the window-shutters, accompanied by the occasional hiss of a stray drop that fell
down the chimney into the fire, and the steady puffing
of the man in the corner, who had now resumed his pipe
of long clay.

The stillness was unexpectedly broken. The distant
sound of a gun reverberated through the air—apparently from the direction of the county-town.

"Be jiggered!" cried the stranger who had sung the
song, jumping up.

"What does that mean?" asked several.

"A prisoner escaped from the jail—that's what it
means."

All listened. The sound was repeated, and none of
them spoke but the man in the chimney-corner, who
said, quietly, "I've often been told that in this county

they fire a gun at such times; but I never heard it till now."

"I wonder if it is *my* man?" murmured the personage in cinder-gray.

"Surely it is!" said the shepherd, involuntarily. "And surely we've seen him! That little man who looked in at the door by now, and quivered like a leaf when he seed ye and heard your song."

"His teeth chattered, and the breath went out of his body," said the dairy-man.

"And his heart seemed to sink within him like a stone," said Oliver Giles.

"And he bolted as if he'd been shot at," said the hedge-carpenter.

"True—his teeth chattered, and his heart seemed to sink; and he bolted as if he'd been shot at," slowly summed up the man in the chimney-corner.

"I didn't notice it," remarked the hangman.

"We were all a-wondering what made him run off in such a fright," faltered one of the women against the wall, "and now 'tis explained."

The firing of the alarm-gun went on at intervals, low and sullenly, and their suspicions became a certainty. The sinister gentleman in cinder-gray roused himself. "Is there a constable here?" he asked, in thick tones. "If so, let him step forward?"

The engaged man of fifty stepped quavering out of the corner, his betrothed beginning to sob on the back of the chair.

"You are a sworn constable?"

"I be, sir."

"Then pursue the criminal at once, with assistance, and bring him back here. He can't have gone far."

"I will, sir, I will—when I've got my staff. I'll go home and get it, and come sharp here, and start in a body."

"Staff!—never mind your staff; the man'll be gone!"

"But I can't do nothing without my staff—can I, William, and John, and Charles Jake? No; for there's the King's royal crown a-painted on en in yaller and gold, and the lion and the unicorn, so as when I raise en up and hit my prisoner, 'tis made a lawful blow thereby. I wouldn't 'tempt to take a man without my staff—no, not I. If I hadn't the law to gie me courage, why, instead o' my taking up him he might take up me!"

"Now, I'm a King's man myself, and can give you authority enough for this," said the formidable officer in gray. "Now then, all of ye, be ready. Have ye any lanterns?"

"Yes—have ye any lanterns?—I demand it!" said the constable.

"And the rest of you able-bodied—"

"Able-bodied men—yes—the rest of ye!" said the constable.

"Have you some good stout staves and pitchforks—"

"Staves and pitchforks—in the name o' the law! And take 'em in yer hands and go in quest, and do as we in authority tell ye!"

Thus aroused, the men prepared to give chase. The evidence was, indeed, though circumstantial, so convincing, that but little argument was needed to show the shepherd's guests that after what they had seen it would look very much like connivance if they did not instantly pursue the unhappy third stranger, who could not as yet have gone more than a few hundred yards over such uneven country.

A shepherd is always well provided with lanterns; and, lighting these hastily, and with hurdle staves in their hands, they poured out of the door, taking a direction along the crest of the hill, away from the town, the rain having fortunately a little abated.

Disturbed by the noise, or possibly by unpleasant dreams of her baptism, the child who had been christened began to cry heart-brokenly in the room overhead. These notes of grief came down through the chinks of the floor to the ears of the women below, who jumped up one by one, and seemed glad of the excuse to ascend and comfort the baby, for the incidents of the last half-hour greatly oppressed them. Thus in the space of two or three minutes the room on the ground-floor was deserted quite.

But it was not for long. Hardly had the sound of footsteps died away when a man returned round the corner of the house from the direction the pursuers had taken. Peeping in at the door, and seeing nobody there, he entered leisurely. It was the stranger of the chimney-corner, who had gone out with the rest. The motive of his return was shown by his helping himself to a cut piece of skimmer-cake that lay on a ledge beside where he had sat, and which he had apparently forgotten to take with him. He also poured out half a cup more mead from the quantity that remained, ravenously eating and drinking these as he stood. He had not finished when another figure came in just as quietly—his friend in cinder-gray.

"Oh—you here?" said the latter, smiling. "I thought you had gone to help in the capture." And this speaker also revealed the object of his return by looking solicitously round for the fascinating mug of old mead.

"And I thought you had gone," said the other, con-
tinuing his skimmer-cake with some effort.

"Well, on second thoughts, I felt there were enough
without me," said the first, confidentially, "and such a
night as it is, too. Besides, 'tis the business o' the Gov-
ernment to take care of its criminals—not mine."

"True; so it is. And I felt as you did, that there were
enough without me."

"I don't want to break my limbs running over the
humps and hollows of this wild country."

"Nor I neither, between you and me."

"These shepherd people are used to it—simple-minded
souls, you know, stirred up to anything in a moment.
They'll have him ready for me before the morning, and
no trouble to me at all."

"They'll have him, and we shall have saved ourselves
all labor in the matter."

"True, true. Well, my way is to Casterbridge; and
'tis as much as my legs will do to take me that far. Going the same way?"

"No, I am sorry to say! I have to get home over
there" (he nodded indefinitely to the right) "and I feel
as you do, that it is quite enough for my legs to do before bedtime.

The other had by this time finished the mead in the
mug, after which, shaking hands heartily at the door,
and wishing each other well, they went their several
ways.

In the mean time the company of pursuers had
reached the end of the hog's-back elevation which dom-
inated this part of the coomb. They had decided on no
particular plan of action; and, finding that the man of
the baleful trade was no longer in their company, they

seemed quite unable to form any such plan now. They descended in all directions down the hill, and straightway several of the party fell into the snare set by Nature for all misguided midnight ramblers over this part of the cretaceous formation. The "lynches," or flint slopes, which belted the escarpment at intervals of a dozen yards, took the less cautious ones unawares, and losing their footing on the rubbly steep, they slid sharply downward, the lanterns rolling from their hands to the bottom, and there lying on their sides till the horn was scorched through.

When they had again gathered themselves together, the shepherd, as the man who knew the country best, took the lead, and guided them round these treacherous inclines. The lanterns, which seemed rather to dazzle their eyes and warn the fugitive, than to assist them in the explorations, were extinguished, due silence was observed; and in this more rational order they plunged into the vale. It was a grassy, briery, moist defile, affording some shelter to any person who had sought it; but the party perambulated it in vain, and ascended on the other side. Here they wandered apart, and after an interval closed together again to report progress. At the second time of closing in they found themselves near a lonely ash, the single tree on this part of the upland, probably sown there by a passing bird some fifty years before. And here, standing a little to one side of the trunk as motionless as the trunk itself, appeared the man they were in quest of, his outline being well defined against the sky beyond. The band noiselessly drew up and faced him.

"Your money or your life!" said the constable, sternly to the still figure.

"No, no," whispered John Pitcher. " 'Tisn't our side ought to say that. That's the doctrine of vagabonds like him, and we be on the side of the law."

"Well, well," replied the constable, impatiently; "I must say something, mustn't I? and if you had all the weight o' this undertaking upon your mind, perhaps you'd say the wrong thing too! Prisoner at the bar, surrender, in the name of the Father—the Crown, I mane!"

The man under the tree seemed now to notice them for the first time, and giving them no opportunity whatever for exhibiting their courage, he strolled slowly towards them. He was, indeed, the little man, the third stranger; but his trepidation had in a great measure gone.

"Well, travellers," he said; "did I hear ye speak to me?"

"You did; you've got to come and be our prisoner at once," said the constable. "We arrest ye on the charge of not biding in Casterbridge jail in a decent proper manner to be hung to-morrow morning. Neighbors, do your duty, and seize the culpet!"

On hearing the charge, the man seemed enlightened, and, saying not another word, resigned himself with preternatural civility to the search party, who, with their staves in their hands, surrounded him on all sides, and marched him back towards the shepherd's cottage.

It was eleven o'clock by the time they arrived. The light shining from the open door, a sound of men's voices within, proclaimed to them as they approached the house that some new events had arisen in their absence. On entering they discovered the shepherd's liv-

ing-room to be invaded by two officers from Casterbridge jail, and a well-known magistrate who lived at
the nearest county-seat, intelligence of the escape having
become generally circulated.

"Gentlemen," said the constable, "I have brought back
your man—not without risk and danger; but every one
must do his duty! He is inside this circle of able-bodied
persons, who have lent me useful aid, considering their
ignorance of Crown work. Men, bring forward your
prisoner!" And the third stranger was led to the light.

"Who is this?" said one of the officials.

"The man," said the constable.

"Certainly not," said the turnkey; and the first cor-
roborated his statement.

"But how can it be otherwise?" asked the constable.
"Or why was he so terrified at sight o' the singing instrument of the law who sat there?" Here he related
the strange behavior of the third stranger on entering
the house during the hangman's song.

"Can't understand it," said the officer, coolly. "All I
know is that it is not the condemned man. He's quite
a different character from this one; a gauntish fellow,
with dark hair and eyes, rather good-looking, and with
a musical bass voice that if you heard it once you'd
never mistake as long as you lived."

"Why, souls—'twas the man in the chimney-corner!"

"Hey—what?" said the magistrate, coming forward
after inquiring particulars from the shepherd in the
background. "Haven't you got the man after all?"

"Well, sir," said the constable, "he's the man we were
in search of, that's true; and yet he's not the man we
were in search of. For the man we were in search of

was not the man we wanted, sir, if you understand my everyday way; for 'twas the man in the chimney-corner!"

"A pretty kettle of fish altogether!" said the magistrate. "You had better start for the other man at once."

The prisoner now spoke for the first time. The mention of the man in the chimney-corner seemed to have moved him as nothing else could do. "Sir," he said, stepping forward to the magistrate, "take no more trouble about me. The time is come when I may as well speak. I have done nothing; my crime is that the condemned man is my brother. Early this afternoon I left home at Shottsford to tramp it all the way to Casterbridge jail to bid him farewell. I was benighted, and called here to rest and ask the way. When I opened the door I saw before me the very man, my brother, that I thought to see in the condemned cell at Casterbridge. He was in this chimney-corner; and jammed close to him, so that he could not have got out if he had tried, was the executioner who'd come to take his life, singing a song about it, and not knowing that it was his victim who was close by, joining in to save appearances. My brother looked a glance of agony at me, and I knew he meant, 'Don't reveal what you see; my life depends on it.' I was so terror-struck that I could hardly stand, and, not knowing what I did, I turned and hurried away."

The narrator's manner and tone had the stamp of truth, and his story made a great impression on all around. "And do you know where your brother is at the present time?" asked the magistrate.

"I do not. I have never seen him since I closed this door."

"I can testify to that, for we've been between ye ever since," said the constable.

"Where does he think to fly to?—what is his occupation?"

"He's a watch and clock maker, sir."

"A said a was a wheelwright—a wicked rogue," said the constable.

"The wheels of clocks and watches he meant, no doubt," said Shepherd Fennel. "I thought his hands was palish for 's trade."

"Well, it appears to me that nothing can be gained by retaining this poor man in custody," said the magistrate. "Your business lies with the other, unquestionably."

And so the little man was released off-hand; but he looked nothing the less sad on that account, it being beyond the power of magistrate or constable to raze out the written troubles in his brain, for they concerned another whom he regarded with more solicitude than himself. When this was done, and the man had gone his way, the night was found to be so far advanced that it was deemed useless to renew the search before the next morning.

Next day, accordingly, the quest for the clever sheep-stealer became general and keen, to all appearance at least. But the intended punishment was cruelly disproportioned to the transgression, and the sympathy of a great many country folk in that district was strongly on the side of the fugitive. Moreover, his marvellous coolness and daring in hob-and-nobbing with the hangman under the unprecedented circumstances of the shepherd's party, won their admiration. So that it may be questioned if all those who ostensibly made themselves so busy in exploring woods and fields and lanes were quite so thorough when it came to the private examination of their own lofts and out-houses. Stories were afloat of a mysterious figure being occasionally seen in some old overgrown track-way or other, remote from turnpike-roads; but when a search was instituted in any of these suspected quarters nobody was found. Thus the days and weeks passed without tidings.

In brief, the bass-voiced man of the chimney-corner was never recaptured. Some said that he went across the sea, others that he did not, but buried himself in the depths of a populous city. At any rate, the gentleman in cinder-gray never did his morning's work at Casterbridge, nor met anywhere at all, for business purposes, the genial comrade with whom he had passed an hour of relaxation in the lonely house on the coomb.

The grass has long been green on the graves of Shepherd Fennel and his frugal wife; the guests who made up the christening-party have mainly followed their entertainers to the tomb; the baby in whose honor they all had met is a matron in the sear and yellow leaf. But the arrival of the three strangers at the shepherd's that night, and the details connected therewith, is a story as well known as ever in the country about Higher Crowstairs.

THE WITHERED ARM

I

A LORN MILKMAID

IT WAS an eighty-cow dairy, and the troop of milkers, regular and supernumerary, were all at work; for, though the time of the year was yet but early April, the feed lay entirely in water-meadows, and the cows were "in full pail." The hour was about six in the evening, and three-fourths of the large, red, rectangular animals having been finished off, there was opportunity for a little conversation.

"He brings home his bride to-morrow, I hear. They've come as far as Anglebury to-day."

The voice seemed to proceed from the belly of the cow called Cherry, but the speaker was a milking-woman, whose face was buried in the flank of that motionless beast.

"Has anybody seen her?" said another.

There was a negative response from the first. "Though they say she's a rosy-cheeked, tisty-tosty little body enough," she added; and as the milkmaid spoke she turned her face so that she could glance past her cow's tail to the other side of the barton, where a thin, faded woman of thirty milked somewhat apart from the rest.

"Years younger than he, they say," continued the second, with also a glance of reflectiveness in the same direction.

"How old do you call him, then?"

"Thirty or so."

"More like forty," broke in an old milkman near, in a long white pinafore or "wropper," and with the brim of his hat tied down so that he looked like a woman.

41

"A was born before our Great Weir was builded, and I hadn't man's wages when I laved water there."

The discussion waxed so warm that the purr of the milk-streams became jerky, till a voice from another cow's belly cried with authority, "Now then, what the Turk do it matter to us about Farmer Lodge's age, or Farmer Lodge's new mis'ess! I shall have to pay him nine pound a year for the rent of every one of these milchers, whatever his age or hers. Get on with your work, or 'twill be dark before we have done. The evening is pinking in a'ready." This speaker was the dairyman himself, by whom the milkmaids and men were employed.

Nothing more was said publicly about Farmer Lodge's wedding, but the first woman murmured, under her cow to her next neighbor, " 'Tis hard for *she*," signifying the thin, worn milkmaid aforesaid.

"Oh, no," said the second. "He hasn't spoke to Rhoda Brook for years."

When the milking was done they washed their pails and hung them on a many-forked stand made of the peeled limb of an oak-tree, set upright in the earth, and resembling a colossal antlered horn. The majority then dispersed in various directions homeward. The thin woman who had not spoken was joined by a boy of twelve or thereabout, and the twain went away up the field also.

Their course lay apart from that of the others, to a lonely spot high above the water-meads, and not far from the border of Egdon Heath, whose dark countenance was visible in the distance as they drew nigh to their home.

"They've just been saying down in barton that your

father brings his young wife home from Anglebury to-morrow," the woman observed. "I shall want to send you for a few things to market, and you'll be pretty sure to meet 'em."

"Yes, mother," said the boy. "Is father married, then?"

"Yes . . . You can give her a look, and tell me what she's like, if you do see her."

"Yes, mother."

"If she's dark or fair, and if she's tall—as tall as I. And if she seems like a woman who has ever worked for a living, or one that has always been well off, and has never done anything, and shows marks of the lady on her, as I expect she do."

"Yes."

They crept up the hill in the twilight, and entered the cottage. It was thatched, and built of mud-walls, the surface of which had been washed by many rains into channels and depressions that left none of the original flat surface visible, while here and there a rafter showed like a bone protruding through the skin.

She was kneeling down in the chimney-corner, before two pieces of turf laid together with the heather inward, blowing at the red-hot ashes with her breath till the turfs flamed. The radiance lit her pale cheek, and made her dark eyes, that had once been handsome, seem handsome anew. "Yes," she resumed, "see if she is dark or fair; and if you can, notice if her hands are white; if not, see if they look as though she had ever done housework, or are milker's hands like mine."

The boy again promised, inattentively this time, his mother not observing that he was cutting a notch with his pocket-knife in the beech-backed chair.

II

THE YOUNG WIFE

The road from Anglebury to Holmstoke is in general level; but there is one place where a sharp ascent breaks its monotony. Farmers homeward-bound from the former market-town, who trot all the rest of the way, walk their horses up this short incline.

The next evening, while the sun was yet bright, a handsome new gig, with a lemon-colored body and red wheels, was spinning westward along the level highway at the heels of a powerful mare. The driver was a yeoman in the prime of life, cleanly shaven like an actor, his face being toned to that bluish-vermilion hue which so often graces a thriving farmer's features when returning home after successful dealings in the town. Beside him sat a woman, many years his junior—almost, indeed, a girl. Her face, too, was fresh in color, but it was of a totally different quality—soft and evanescent, like the light under a heap of rose-petals.

Few people travelled this way, for it was not a turn-pike-road; and the long white ribbon of gravel that stretched before them was empty, save of one small scarce-moving speck, which presently resolved itself into the figure of a boy, who was creeping on at a snail's pace, and continually looking behind him—the heavy bundle he carried being some excuse for, if not the reason of, his dilatoriness. When the bouncing gig-party slowed at the bottom of the incline before mentioned, the pedestrian was only a few yards in front. Supporting the large bundle by putting one hand on his hip, he turned and looked straight at the farmer's wife as though he would read her through and through, pacing along abreast of the horse.

The low sun was full in her face, rendering every feature, shade, and contour distinct, from the curve of her little nostril to the color of her eyes. The farmer, though he seemed annoyed at the boy's persistent presence, did not order him to get out of the way; and thus the lad preceded them, his hard gaze never leaving her; till they reached the top of the ascent, when the farmer trotted on with relief in his lineaments—having taken no outward notice of the boy whatever.

"How that poor lad stared at me!" said the young wife.

"Yes, dear; I saw that he did."

"He is one of the village, I suppose?"

"One of the neighborhood. I think he lives with his mother a mile or two off."

"He knows who we are, no doubt?"

"Oh, yes. You must expect to be stared at just at first, my pretty Gertrude."

"I do—though I think the poor boy may have looked at us in the hope that we might relieve him of his heavy load, rather than from curiosity."

"Oh, no," said her husband, off-handedly. "These country lads will carry a hundred-weight once they get it on their backs; besides, his pack had more size than weight in it. Now, then, another mile and I shall be able to show you our house in the distance—if it is not too dark before we get there." The wheels spun round, and particles flew from their periphery as before, till a white house of ample dimensions revealed itself, with farm-buildings and ricks at the back.

Meanwhile the boy had quickened his pace, and turn-

ing up a by-lane some mile and a half short of the white
farmstead, ascended towards the leaner pastures, and
so on to the cottage of his mother.

She had reached home after her day's milking at the
outlying dairy, and was washing cabbage at the door-
way in the declining light. "Hold up the net a moment,"
she said, without preface, as the boy came up.

He flung down his bundle, held the edge of the cab-
bage-net, and as she filled its meshes with the dripping
leaves she went on: "Well, did you see her?"

"Yes, quite plain."

"Is she lady-like?"

"Yes; and more. A lady complete."

"Is she young?"

"Well, she's growed up, and her ways are quite a
woman's."

"Of course. What color is her hair and face?"

"Her hair is lightish, and her face as comely as a
live doll's."

"Her eyes, then, are not dark like mine?"

"No—of a bluish turn; and her mouth is very nice
and red, and when she smiles her teeth show white."

"Is she tall?" said the woman, sharply.

"I couldn't see. She was sitting down."

"Then do you go to Holmstoke Church to-morrow
morning—she's sure to be there. Go early and notice
her walking in, and come home and tell me if she's
taller than I."

"Very well, mother. But why don't you go and see
for yourself?"

"*I* go to see her! I wouldn't look up at her if she were
to pass my window this instant. She was with Mr.
Lodge, of course? What did he say or do?"

"Just the same as usual."

"Took no notice of you?"

"None."

Next day the mother put a clean shirt on the boy and started him off for Holmstoke Church. He reached the ancient little pile, when the door was just being opened, and he was the first to enter. Taking his seat by the font, he watched all the parishioners file in. The well-to-do Farmer Lodge came nearly last; and his young wife, who accompanied him, walked up the aisle with the shyness natural to a modest woman who had appeared thus for the first time. As all other eyes were fixed upon her, the youth's stare was not noticed now.

When he reached home his mother said "Well?" before he had entered the room.

"She is not tall. She is rather short," he replied.

"Ah!" said his mother, with satisfaction.

"But she's very pretty—very. In fact, she's lovely." The youthful freshness of the yeoman's wife had evidently made an impression even on the somewhat hard nature of the boy.

"That's all I want to hear," said his mother, quickly. "Now spread the table-cloth. The hare you caught is very tender; but mind that nobody catches you. You've never told me what sort of hands she had."

"I have never seen 'em. She never took off her gloves."

"What did she wear this morning?"

"A white bonnet and a silver-colored gownd. It whewed and whistled so loud when it rubbed against the pews that the lady colored up more than ever for very shame at the noise, and pulled it in to keep it from touching; but when she pushed into her seat it whewed more than ever. Mr. Lodge, he seemed pleased, and his waistcoat stuck out, and his great golden seals hung like a lord's; but she seemed to wish her noisy gownd anywhere but on her."

"Not she! However, that will do now."

These descriptions of the newly married couple were continued from time to time by the boy at his mother's request, after any chance encounter he had had with them. But Rhoda Brook, though she might easily have seen young Mrs. Lodge for herself by walking a couple of miles, would never attempt an excursion towards the quarter where the farm-house lay. Neither did she, at the daily milking in the dairy-man's yard on Lodge's outlying second farm, ever speak on the subject of the recent marriage. The dairy-man, who rented the cows of Lodge, and knew perfectly the tall milkmaid's history, with manly kindliness always kept the gossip in the cow-barton from annoying Rhoda. But the atmosphere thereabout was full of the subject during the first days of Mrs. Lodge's arrival; and from her boy's description and the casual words of the other milkers, Rhoda Brook could raise a mental image of the unconscious Mrs. Lodge that was realistic as a photograph.

III

A VISION

One night, two or three weeks after the bridal return, when the boy was gone to bed, Rhoda sat a long time over the turf-ashes that she had raked out in front of her to extinguish them. She contemplated so intently the new wife, as presented to her in her mind's eye, over the embers, that she forgot the lapse of time. At last, wearied with her day's work, she too retired.

But the figure which had occupied her so much during this and the previous days was not to be banished at night. For the first time Gertrude Lodge visited the supplanted woman in her dreams. Rhoda Brook dreamed—since her assertion that she really saw, before falling asleep, was not to be believed—that the young wife, in the pale silk dress and white bonnet, but with features shockingly distorted, and wrinkled as by age, was sitting upon her chest as she lay. The pressure of Mrs. Lodge's person grew heavier; the blue eyes peered cruelly into her face; and then the figure thrust forward its left hand mockingly, so as to make the wedding-ring it wore glitter in Rhoda's eyes. Maddened mentally, and nearly suffocated by pressure, the sleeper struggled; the incubus, still regarding her, withdrew to the foot of the bed, only, however, to come forward by degrees, resume her seat, and flash her left hand as before.

Gasping for breath, Rhoda, in a last desperate effort, swung out her right hand, seized the confronting spectre by its obtrusive left arm, and whirled it backward to the floor, starting up herself as she did so, with a low cry.

"Oh, merciful Heaven!" she cried, sitting on the edge of the bed in a cold sweat, "that was not a dream —she was here!"

She could feel her antagonist's arm within her grasp even now—the very flesh and bone of it, as it seemed. She looked on the floor whither she had whirled the spectre, but there was nothing to be seen.

Rhoda Brook slept no more that night, and when she went milking at the next dawn they noticed how pale and haggard she looked. The milk that she drew quivered into her pail; her hand had not calmed even yet, and still retained the feel of the arm. She came home to breakfast as wearily as if it had been supper-time.

"What was that noise in your chimmer, mother, last night?" said her son. "You fell off the bed, surely?"

"Did you hear anything fall? At what time?"

"Just when the clock struck two."

She could not explain, and when the meal was done went silently about her housework, the boy assisting her, for he hated going afield on the farms, and she indulged his reluctance. Between eleven and twelve the garden gate clicked, and she lifted her eyes to the window. At the bottom of the garden, within the gate, stood the woman of her vision. Rhoda seemed trans-fixed.

"Ah, she said she would come!" exclaimed the boy, also observing her.

"Said so—when? How does she know us?"

"I have seen and spoken to her. I talked to her yesterday."

"I told you," said the mother, flushing indignantly, "never to speak to anybody in that house, or go near the place."

"I did not speak to her till she spoke to me. And I did not go near the place. I met her in the road."

"What did you tell her?"

"Nothing. She said, 'Are you the poor boy who had to bring the heavy load from market?' And she looked at my boots, and said they would not keep my feet dry if it came on wet, because they were so cracked. I told her I lived with my mother, and we had enough to do to keep ourselves, and that's how it was; and she said then, 'I'll come and bring you some better boots, and see your mother.' She gives away things to other folks in the meads besides us."

Mrs. Lodge was by this time close to the door—not in her silk, as Rhoda had seen her in the bedchamber, but in a morning hat, and gown of common light material, which became her better than silk. On her arm she carried a basket.

The impression remaining from the night's experience was still strong. Rhoda had almost expected to see the wrinkles, the scorn, and the cruelty on her visitor's face. She would have escaped an interview, had escape been possible. There was, however, no back door to the cottage, and in an instant the boy had lifted the latch to Mrs. Lodge's gentle knock.

"I see I have come to the right house," said she, glancing at the lad, and smiling. "But I was not sure till you opened the door."

The figure and action were those of the phantom; but her voice was so indescribably sweet, her glance so winning, her smile so tender, so unlike that of Rhoda's midnight visitant, that the latter could hardly believe the evidence of her senses. She was truly glad that she had not hidden away in sheer aversion, as she had been inclined to do. In her basket Mrs. Lodge brought the pair of boots that she had promised to the boy, and other useful articles.

At these proofs of a kindly feeling towards her and hers, Rhoda's heart reproached her bitterly. This innocent young thing should have her blessing and not her curse. When she left them, a light seemed gone from the dwelling. Two days later she came again to

know if the boots fitted; and less than a fortnight after
that paid Rhoda another call. On this occasion the
boy was absent.

"I walk a good deal," said Mrs. Lodge, "and your
house is the nearest outside our own parish. I hope
you are well. You don't look quite well."

Rhoda said she was well enough; and indeed, though
the paler of the two, there was more of the strength
that endures in her well-defined features and large
frame than in the soft-cheeked young woman before
her. The conversation became quite confidential as
regarded their powers and weaknesses; and when Mrs.
Lodge was leaving, Rhoda said, "I hope you will find
this air agree with you, ma'am, and not suffer from
the damp of the water-meads."

The younger one replied that there was not much
doubt of it, her general health being usually good.
"Though, now you remind me," she added, "I have
one little ailment which puzzles me. It is nothing
serious, but I cannot make it out."

She uncovered her left hand and arm; and their
outline confronted Rhoda's gaze as the exact original
of the limb she had beheld and seized in her dream.
Upon the pink round surface of the arm were faint
marks of an unhealthy color, as if produced by a rough
grasp. Rhoda's eyes became riveted on the discolora-
tions; she fancied that she discerned in them the shape
of her own four fingers.

"How did it happen?" she said, mechanically.

"I cannot tell," replied Mrs. Lodge, shaking her
head. "One night when I was sound asleep, dreaming
I was away in some strange place, a pain suddenly shot
into my arm there, and was so keen as to awaken me.

I must have struck it in the daytime, I suppose, though I don't remember doing so." She added laughing, "I tell my dear husband that it looks just as if he had flown into a rage and struck me there. Oh, I dare say it will soon disappear."

"Ha, ha! Yes! On what night did it come?"

Mrs. Lodge considered, and said it would be a fortnight ago on the morrow. "When I awoke I could not remember where I was," she added, "till the clock striking two reminded me."

She had named the night and the hour of Rhoda's spectral encounter, and Brook felt like a guilty thing. The artless disclosure startled her; she did not reason on the freaks of coincidence; and all the scenery of that ghastly night returned with double vividness to her mind.

"Oh, can it be," she said to herself, when her visitor had departed, "that I exercise a malignant power over people against my own will?" She knew that she had been slyly called a witch since her fall; but never having understood why that particular stigma had been attached to her, it had passed disregarded. Could this be the explanation and had such things as this ever happened before?

IV

A SUGGESTION

The summer drew on, and Rhoda Brook almost dreaded to meet Mrs. Lodge again, notwithstanding that her feeling for the young wife amounted wellnigh to affection. Something in her own individuality seemed to convict Rhoda of crime. Yet a fatality sometimes would direct the steps of the latter to the

outskirts of Holmstoke whenever she left her house
for any other purpose than her daily work; and hence
it happened that their next encounter was out-of-doors.
Rhoda could not avoid the subject which had so mys-
tified her, and after the first few words she stammered,
"I hope your—arm is well again, ma'am?" She had
perceived with consternation that Gertrude Lodge
carried her left arm stiffly.

"No; it is not quite well. Indeed it is no better at all;
it is rather worse. It pains me dreadfully sometimes."

"Perhaps you had better go to a doctor, ma'am."

She replied that she had already seen a doctor. Her
husband had insisted upon her going to one. But the
surgeon had not seemed to understand the afflicted
limb at all; he had told her to bathe it in hot water,
and she had bathed it, but the treatment had done no
good.

"Will you let me see it?" said the milkwoman.

Mrs. Lodge pushed up her sleeve and disclosed the
place, which was a few inches above the wrist. As
soon as Rhoda Brook saw it she could hardly preserve
her composure. There was nothing of the nature of a
wound, but the arm at that point had a shrivelled look,
and the outline of the four fingers appeared more distinct than at the former time. Moreover, she fancied
that they were imprinted in precisely the relative
position of her clutch upon the arm in the trance;
the first finger towards Gertrude's wrist, and the fourth
towards her elbow.

What the impress resembled seemed to have struck
Gertrude herself since their last meeting. "It looks
almost like finger-marks," she said, adding, with a
faint laugh, "My husband says it is as if some witch,

or the devil himself, had taken hold of me there, and blasted the flesh."

Rhoda shivered. "That's fancy," she said hurriedly. "I wouldn't mind it, if I were you."

"I shouldn't so much mind it," said the younger, with hesitation, "if—if I hadn't a notion that it makes my husband—dislike me—no, love me less. Men think so much of personal appearance."

"Some do—he for one."

"Yes; and he was very proud of mine, at first."

"Keep your arm covered from his sight."

"Ah, he knows the disfigurement is there!" She tried to hide the tears that filled her eyes.

"Well, ma'am, I earnestly hope it will go away soon."

And so the milkwoman's mind was chained anew to the subject by a horrid sort of spell as she returned home. The sense of having been guilty of an act of malignity increased, affect as she might to ridicule her superstition. In her secret heart Rhoda did not altogether object to a slight diminution of her successor's beauty, by whatever means it had come about; but she did not wish to inflict upon her physical pain. For though this pretty young woman had rendered impossible any reparation which Lodge might have made Rhoda for his past conduct, everything like resentment at the unconscious usurpation had quite passed away from the elder's mind.

If the sweet and kindly Gertrude Lodge only knew of the scene in the bedchamber, what would she think? Not to inform her of it seemed treachery in the presence of her friendliness; but tell she could not of her own accord, neither could she devise a remedy.

She mused upon the matter the greater part of the

night; and the next day, after the morning milking, set out to obtain another glimpse of Gertrude Lodge if she could, being held to her by a grewsome fascination. By watching the house from a distance the milkmaid was presently able to discern the farmer's wife in a ride she was taking alone; probably to join her husband in some distant field. Mrs. Lodge perceived her, and cantered in her direction.

"Good morning, Rhoda!" Gertrude said, when she had come up. "I was going to call."

Rhoda noticed that Mrs. Lodge held the reins with some difficulty.

"I hope—the bad arm," said Rhoda.

"They tell me there is possibly one way by which I might be able to find out the cause, and so perhaps the cure of it," replied the other, anxiously. "It is by going to some clever man over in Egdon Heath. They did not know if he was still alive—and I cannot remember his name at this moment; but they said that you knew more of his movements than anybody else hereabout, and could tell me if he were still to be consulted. Dear me—what was his name? But you know."

"Not Conjurer Trendle?" said her thin companion, turning pale.

"Trendle—yes. Is he alive?"

"I believe so," said Rhoda, with reluctance.

"Why do you call him conjurer?"

"Well—they say—they used to say he was a—he had powers other folks have not."

"Oh, how could my people be so superstitious as to recommend a man of that sort? I thought they meant some medical man. I shall think no more of him."

Rhoda looked relieved, and Mrs. Lodge rode on.

The milkwoman had inwardly seen, from the moment she heard of her having been mentioned as a reference for this man, that there must exist a sarcastic feeling among the work-folk that a sorceress would know the whereabouts of the exorcist.   They suspected her, then.   A short time ago this would have given no concern to a woman of her common-sense.   But she had a haunting reason to be superstitious now; and she had been seized with sudden dread that this Conjurer Trendle might name her as the malignant influence which was blasting the fair person of Gertrude, and so lead her friend to hate her forever, and to treat her as some fiend in human shape.

But all was not over.   Two days after, a shadow intruded into the window-pattern thrown on Rhoda Brook's floor by the afternoon sun.   The woman opened the door at once, almost breathlessly.

"Are you alone?" said Gertrude.   She seemed to be no less harassed and anxious than Brook herself.

"Yes," said Rhoda.

"The place on my arm seems worse, and troubles me!" the farmer's wife went on.   "It is so mysterious! I do hope it will not be a permanent blemish.   I have again been thinking of what they said about Conjurer Trendle.   I don't really believe in such men, but I should not mind just visiting him, from curiosity— though on no account must my husband know.   Is it far to where he lives?"

"Yes—five miles," said Rhoda, backwardly.   "In the heart of Egdon."

"Well, I should have to walk.   Could you not go with me to show me the way—say to-morrow afternoon?"

"Oh, not I—that is," the milkwoman murmured, with a start of dismay. Again the dread seized her that something to do with her fierce act in the dream might be revealed, and her character in the eyes of the most useful friend she had ever had be ruined irretrievably.

Mrs. Lodge urged, and Rhoda finally assented, though with much misgiving. Sad as the journey would be to her, she could not conscientiously stand in the way of a possible remedy for her patron's strange affliction. It was agreed that, to escape suspicion of their mystic intent, they should meet at the edge of the heath, at the corner of a plantation which was visible from the spot where they now stood.

V

CONJURER TRENDLE

By the next afternoon Rhoda would have done anything to escape this inquiry. But she had promised to go. Moreover, there was a horrid fascination at times in becoming instrumental in throwing such possible light on her own character as would reveal her to be something greater in the occult world than she had ever herself suspected.

She started just before the time of day mentioned between them, and half an hour's brisk walking brought her to the south-eastern extension of the Egdon tract of country, where the fir plantation was. A slight figure, cloaked and veiled, was already there. Rhoda recognized, almost with a shudder, that Mrs. Lodge bore her left arm in a sling.

They heardly spoke to each other, and immediately set out on their climb into the interior of this solemn country, which stood high above the rich alluvial soil they had left half an hour before. It was a long walk; thick clouds made the atmosphere dark, though it was as yet only early afternoon; and the wind howled dismally over the hills of the heath—not improbably the same heath which had witnessed the agony of the Wessex King Ina, presented to after-ages as Lear. Gertrude Lodge talked most, Rhoda replying with monosyllabic preoccupation. She had a strange dislike to walking on the side of her companion where hung the afflicted arm, moving round to the other when inadvertently near it. Much heather had been brushed by their feet when they descended upon a cart-track, beside which stood the house of the man they sought.

He did not profess his remedial practices openly, or care anything about their continuance, his direct interests being those of a dealer in furze, turf, "sharp sand," and other local products. Indeed, he affected not to believe largely in his own powers, and when warts that had been shown him for cure miraculously disappeared—which it must be owned they infallibly did—he would say lightly, "Oh, I only drink a glass of grog upon 'em—perhaps it's all chance," and immediately turn the subject.

He was at home when they arrived, having, in fact, seen them descending into his valley. He was a gray-bearded man, with a reddish face, and he looked singularly at Rhoda the first moment he beheld her. Mrs. Lodge told him her errand, and then with words of self-disparagement he examined her arm.

"Medicine can't cure it," he said, promptly, " 'Tis the work of an enemy."

Rhoda shrank into herself and drew back.

"An enemy? What enemy?" asked Mrs. Lodge.

He shook his head. "That's best known to yourself," he said. "If you like I can show the person to you, though I shall not myself know who it is. I can do no more, and don't wish to do that."

She pressed him; on which he told Rhoda to wait outside where she stood, and took Mrs. Lodge into the room. It opened immediately from the door; and, as the latter remained ajar, Rhoda Brook could see the proceedings without taking part in them. He brought a tumbler from the dresser, nearly filled it with water, and fetching an egg, prepared it in some private way; after which he broke it on the edge of the glass, so that the white went in and the yolk remained. As it was getting gloomy, he took the glass and its contents to the window, and told Gertrude to watch them closely. They leaned over the table together, and the milkwoman could see the opaline hue of the egg-fluid changing form as it sank in the water, but she was not near enough to define the shape that it assumed.

"Do you catch the likeness of any face or figure as you look?" demanded the conjurer of the young woman.

She murmured a reply, in tones so low as to be inaudible to Rhoda, and continued to gaze intently into the glass. Rhoda turned, and walked a few steps away.

When Mrs. Lodge came out, and her face was met by the light, it appeared exceedingly pale—as pale as Rhoda's—against the sad dun shades of the upland's garniture. Trendle shut the door behind her, and they at once started homeward together. But Rhoda perceived that her companion had quite changed.

"Did he charge much?" she asked, tentatively.

"Oh no—nothing. He would not take a farthing," said Gertrude.

"And what did you see?" inquired Rhoda.

"Nothing I—care to speak of." The constraint in her manner was remarkable; her face was so rigid as to wear an oldened aspect, faintly suggestive of the face in Rhoda's bedchamber.

"Was it you who first proposed coming here?" Mrs. Lodge suddenly inquired, after a long pause. "How very odd, if you did!"

"No. But I am not sorry we have come, all things considered," she replied. For the first time a sense of triumph possessed her, and she did not altogether deplore that the young thing at her side should learn that their lives had been antagonized by other influences than their own.

The subject was no more alluded to during the long and dreary walk home. But in some way or other a story was whispered about the many-dairied Swenn Valley that winter that Mrs. Lodge's gradual loss of the use of her left arm was owing to her being "overlooked" by Rhoda Brook. The latter kept her own counsel about the incubus, but her face grew sadder and thinner; and in the spring she and her boy disappeared from the neighborhood of Holmstoke.

VI

A SECOND ATTEMPT

Half a dozen years passed away, and Mr. and Mrs. Lodge's married experience sank into prosiness, and worse. The farmer was usually gloomy and silent; the woman whom he had wooed for her grace and beauty was contorted and disfigured in the left limb; moreover, she had brought him no child, which rendered it likely that he would be the last of a family who had occupied that valley for some two hundred years. He thought of Rhoda Brook and her son, and feared this might be a judgment from Heaven upon him.

The once blithe-hearted and enlightened Gertrude was changing into an irritable, superstitious woman, whose whole time was given to experimenting upon her ailment with every quack remedy she came across. She was honestly attached to her husband, and was ever secretly hoping against hope to win back his heart again by regaining some at least of her personal beauty. Hence it arose that her closet was lined with bottles, packets, and ointment-pots of every description—nay, bunches of mystic herbs, charms, and books of necromancy, which in her school-girl times she would have ridiculed as folly.

"D—d if you won't poison yourself with these apothecary messes and witch mixtures some time or other," said her husband, when his eye chanced to fall upon the multitudinous array.

She did not reply, but turned her sad, soft glance upon him in such heart-swollen reproach that he looked sorry for his words, and added, "I only meant it for your good, you know, Gertrude."

"I'll clear out the whole lot, and destroy them," said she, huskily, "and attempt such remedies no more!"

"You want somebody to cheer you," he observed. "I once thought of adopting a boy; but he is too old now. And he is gone away I don't know where."

She guessed to whom he alluded; for Rhoda Brook's story had in the course of years become known to her; though not a word had ever passed between her husband and herself on the subject. Neither had she ever spoken to him of her visit to Conjurer Trendle, and of what was revealed to her, or she thought was revealed to her, by that solitary heath-man.

She was now five-and-twenty; but she seemed older. "Six years of marriage, and only a few months of love," she sometimes whispered to herself. And then she thought of the apparent cause, and said, with a tragic glance at her withering limb, "If I could only again be as I was when he first saw me!"

She obediently destroyed her nostrums and charms; but there remained a hankering wish to try something else—some other sort of cure altogether. She had never revisited Trendle since she had been conducted to the house of the solitary by Rhoda against her will; but it now suddenly occurred to Gertrude that she would, in a last desperate effort at deliverance from this seeming curse, again seek out the man, if he yet lived. He was entitled to a certain credence, for the indistinct form he had raised in the glass had undoubtedly resembled the only woman in the world who—as she now knew, though not then—could have a reason for bearing her ill-will. The visit should be paid.

This time she went alone, though she nearly got lost on the heath, and roamed a considerable distance out

of her way. Trendle's house was reached at last, however; he was not in-doors, and instead of waiting at
the cottage she went to where his bent figure was
pointed out to her at work a long way off. Trendle
remembered her, and laying down the handful of
furze-roots which he was gathering and throwing into
a heap, he offered to accompany her in her homeward
direction, as the distance was considerable and the days
were short. So they walked together, his head bowed
nearly to the earth, and his form of a color with it.

"You can send away warts and other excrescences,
I know," she said; "why can't you send away this?"
And the arm was uncovered.

"You think too much of my powers!" said Trendle;
"and I am old and weak now, too. No, no; it is too
much for me to attempt in my own person. What have
ye tried?"

She named to him some of the hundred medicaments
and counter-spells which she had adopted from time
to time. He shook his head.

"Some were good enough," he said, approvingly;
"but not many of them for such as this. This is of
the nature of a blight, not of the nature of a wound;
and if you ever do throw it off, it will be all at once."

"If I only could!"

"There is only one chance of doing it known to me.
It has never failed in kindred afflictions—that I can
declare. But it is hard to carry out, and especially
for a woman."

"Tell me!" said she.

"You must touch with the limb the neck of a man
who's been hanged."

She started a little at the image he had raised.

"Before he's cold—just after he's cut down," continued the conjurer, impassively.

"How can that do good?"

"It will turn the blood and change the constitution. But, as I say, to do it is hard. You must get into jail, and wait for him when he's brought off the gallows. Lots have done it, though perhaps not such pretty women as you. I used to send dozens for skin complaints. But that was in former times. The last I sent was in '13—near twenty years ago."

He had no more to tell her; and when he had put her into a straight track homeward, turned and left her, refusing all money, as at first.

VII

A RIDE

The communication sank deep into Gertrude's mind. Her nature was rather a timid one; and probably of all remedies that the white wizard could have suggested there was not one which would have filled her with so much aversion as this, not to speak of the immense obstacles in the way of its adoption.

Casterbridge, the county-town, was a dozen or fifteen miles off; and though in those days, when men were executed for horse-stealing, arson, and burglary, an assize seldom passed without a hanging, it was not likely that she could get access to the body of the criminal unaided. And the fear of her husband's anger made her reluctant to breathe a word of Trendle's suggestion to him or to anybody about him.

She did nothing for months, and patiently bore her disfigurement as before. But her woman's nature,

craving for renewed love, through the medium of renewed beauty (she was but twenty-five), was ever
stimulating her to try what, at any rate, could hardly
do her any harm. "What came by a spell will go by
a spell surely," she would say. Whenever her imagination pictured the act she shrank in terror from the pos-
sibility of it; then the words of the conjurer, "It will
turn your blood," were seen to be capable of a scientific
no less than a ghastly interpretation; the mastering
desire returned, and urged her on again.

There was at this time but one county-paper, and
that her husband only occasionally borrowed. But
old-fashioned days had old-fashioned means, and news
was extensively conveyed by word of mouth from
market to market or from fair to fair; so that, whenever such an event as an execution was about to take
place, few within a radius of twenty miles were ignor-
ant of the coming sight; and, so far as Holmstoke was
concerned, some enthusiasts had been known to walk
all the way to Casterbridge and back in one day, solely
to witness the spectacle. The next assizes were in
March; and when Gertrude Lodge heard that they had
been held, she inquired steathily at the inn as to the
result, as soon as she could find opportunity.

She was, however, too late. The time at which the
sentences were to be carried out had arrived, and to
make the journey and obtain admission at such short
notice required at least her husband's assistance. She
dared not tell him, for she had found by delicate experiment that these smouldering village beliefs made
him furious if mentioned, partly because he half en-
tertained them himself. It was therefore necessary to
wait for another opportunity.

Her determination received a fillip from learning that two epileptic children had attended from this very village of Holmstoke many years before with beneficial results, though the experiment had been strongly condemned by the neighboring clergy. April, May, June passed; and it is no overstatement to say that by the end of the last-named month Gertrude wellnigh longed for the death of a fellow-creature.

Instead of her formal prayers each night, her unconscious prayer was, "O Lord, hang some guilty or innocent person soon!" This time she made earlier inquiries, and was altogether more systematic in her proceedings. Moreover, the season was summer, between the haymaking and the harvest, and in the leisure thus afforded her husband had been holiday-taking away from home.

The assizes were in July, and she went to the inn as before. There was to be one execution—only one, for arson.

Her greatest problem was not how to get to Casterbridge, but what means she could adopt for obtaining admission to the jail. Though access for such purposes had formerly never been denied, the custom had fallen into desuetude; and in contemplating her possible difficulties she was again almost driven to fall back upon her husband. But, on sounding him about the assizes, he was so uncommunicative, so more than usually cold, that she did not proceed, and decided that whatever she did she would do alone.

Fortune, obdurate hitherto, showed her unexpected favor. On the Thursday before the Saturday fixed for the execution, Lodge remarked to her that he was going away from home for another day or two on business at a fair, and that he was sorry he could not take her with him.

She exhibited on this occasion so much readiness to stay at home that he looked at her in surprise. Time had been when she would have shown deep disappointment at the loss of such a jaunt. However, he lapsed into his usual taciturnity, and on the day named left Holmstoke.

It was now her turn. She at first had thought of driving, but on reflection held that driving would not do, since it would necessitate her keeping to the turn-pike-road, and so increase by tenfold the risk of her ghastly errand being found out. She decided to ride, and avoid the beaten track, notwithstanding that in her husband's stables there was no animal just at present which by any stretch of imagination could be consid-ered a lady's mount, in spite of his promise before marriage to always keep a mare for her. He had, however, many horses, fine ones of their kind; and among the rest was a serviceable creature, an equine Amazon, with a back as broad as a sofa, on which Gertrude had occasionally taken an airing when un-well. This horse she chose.

On Friday afternoon one of the men brought it round. She was dressed, and before going down looked at her shrivelled arm. "Ah!" she said to it, "if it had not been for you this terrible ordeal would have been saved me!"

When strapping up the bundle in which she carried a few articles of clothing, she took occasion to say to the servant, "I take these in case I should not get back to-night from the person I am going to visit. Don't be alarmed if I am not in by ten, and close up the house as usual. I shall be at home to-morrow for certain." She meant then to privately tell her husband; the deed accomplished was not like the deed projected. He would almost certainly forgive her.

And then the pretty palpitating Gertrude Lodge went from her husband's homestead; but though her goal was Casterbridge, she did not take the direct route thither through Stickleford. Her cunning course at first was in precisely the opposite direction. As soon as she was out of sight, however, she turned to the left, by a road which led into Egdon, and on entering the heath wheeled round, and set out in the true course, due westerly. A more private way down the county could not be imagined; and as to direction, she had merely to keep her horse's head to a point a little to the right of the sun. She knew that she would light upon a furze-cutter or cottager of some sort from time to time, from whom she might correct her bearing.

Though the date was comparatively recent, Egdon was much less fragmentary in character than now. The attempts—successful and otherwise—at cultivation on the lower slopes, which intrude and break up the original heath into small detached heaths, had not been carried far; Enclosure Acts had not taken effect, and the banks and fences which now exclude the cattle of those villagers who formerly enjoyed rights of commonage thereon, and the carts of those who had turbary privileges which kept them in firing all the year round, were not erected. Gertrude therefore rode along with no other obstacles than the prickly furze-bushes, the mats of heather, the white watercourses, and the natural steeps and declivities of the ground.

Her horse was sure, if heavy-footed and slow, and

though a draught animal, was easy-paced; had it been otherwise, she was not a woman who could have ventured to ride over such a bit of country with a half-dead arm. It was therefore nearly eight-o'clock when she drew rein to breathe the mare on the last outlying high point of heath-land towards Casterbridge, previous to leaving Egdon for the cultivated valleys.

She halted before a pond flanked by the ends of two hedges; a railing ran through the centre of the pond, dividing it in half. Over the railing she saw the low green country; over the green trees the roofs of the town; over the roofs a white, flat façade, denoting the entrance to the county-jail. On the roof of this front specks were moving about; they seemed to be workmen erecting something. Her flesh crept. She descended slowly, and was soon amid cornfields and pastures. In another half-hour, when it was almost dusk, Gertrude reached the White Hart, the first inn of the town on that side.

Little surprise was excited by her arrival: farmers' wives rode on horseback then more than they do now—though, for that matter, Mrs. Lodge was not imagined to be a wife at all; the inn-keeper supposed her some harum-scarum young woman who had come to attend "hang-fair" next day. Neither her husband nor herself ever dealt in Casterbridge market, so that she was unknown. While dismounting she beheld a crowd of boys standing at the door of a harness-maker's shop just above the inn, looking inside it with deep interest.

"What is going on there?" she asked of the hostler.

"Making the rope for to-morrow."

She throbbed responsively, and contracted her arm. " 'Tis sold by the inch afterwards," the man continued. "I could get you a bit, miss, for nothing, if you'd like?"

She hastily repudiated any such wish, all the more from a curious creeping feeling that the condemned wretch's destiny was becoming interwoven with her own; and having engaged a room for the night, sat down to think.

Up to this time she had formed but the vaguest notions about her means of obtaining access to the prison. The words of the cunning man returned to her mind. He had implied that she should use her beauty, impaired though it was, as a pass-key. In her inexperience she knew little about jail functionaries; she had heard of a high-sheriff and an under-sheriff, but dimly only. She knew, however, that there must be a hangman, and to the hangman she determined to apply.

VIII

A WATER-SIDE HERMIT

At this date, and for several years after, there was a hangman to almost every jail. Gertrude found, on inquiry, that the Casterbridge official dwelt in a lonely cottage by a deep, slow river flowing under the cliff on which the prison buildings were situate—the stream being the self-same one, though she did not know it, which watered the Stickleford and Holmstoke meads lower down in its course.

Having changed her dress, and before she had eaten or drunk—for she could not take her ease till she had ascertained some particulars—Gertrude pursued her way by a path along the water-side to the cottage indicated. Passing thus the outskirts of the jail, she

discerned on the level roof over the gate-way three
rectangular lines against the sky, where the specks
had been moving in her distant view; she recognized
what the erection was, and passed quickly on. Another
hundred yards brought her to the executioner's house,
which a boy pointed out. It stood close to the same
stream, and was hard by a weir, the waters of which
emitted a steady roar.

While she stood hesitating, a door opened and an
old man came forth, shading a candle with one hand.
Locking the door on the outside, he turned to a flight
of wooden steps fixed against the end of the cottage,
and began to ascend them, this being evidently the
staircase to his bedroom. Gertrude hastened forward,
but by the time she reached the foot of the ladder he
was at the top. She called to him loudly enough to be
heard above the roar of the weir; he looked down and
said, "What d'ye want here?"

"To speak to you a minute."

The candlelight, such as it was, fell upon her implor-
ing, pale, upturned face, and Davies (as the hangman
was called) backed down the ladder. "I was just going
to bed," he said; " 'Early to bed and early to rise,'
but I don't mind stopping a minute for such a one as
you. Come into the house." He reopened the door,
and preceded her to the room within.

The implements of his daily work, which was that
of a jobbing gardener, stood in a corner, and seeing
probably that she looked rural, he said, "If you want
me to undertake country work I can't come, for I never
leave Casterbridge for gentle nor simple—not I.
Though sometimes I make others leave," he added,
formally.

"Yes, yes! That's it! To-morrow!"

"Ah! I thought so. Well, what's the matter about that? 'Tis no use to come here about the knot—folks do come continually, but I tell 'em one knot is as merciful as another if ye keep it under the ear. Is the unfortunate man a relation; or, I should say, perhaps" (looking at her dress), "a person who's been in your employ?"

"No. What time is the execution?"

"The same as usual—twelve o'clock, or as soon after as the London mail-coach gets in. We always wait for that, in case of a reprieve."

"Oh—a reprieve—I hope not!" she said, involuntarily.

"Well—he, he!—as a matter of business, so do I! But still, if ever a young fellow deserved to be let off, this one does; only just turned eighteen, and only present by chance when the rick was fired. Howsomeever, there's not much risk of it, as they are obliged to make an example of him, there having been so much destruction of property that way lately."

"I mean," she explained, "that I want to touch him for a charm, a cure of an affliction, by the advice of a man who has proved the virtue of the remedy."

"Oh yes, miss! Now I understand. I've had such people come in past years. But it didn't strike me that you looked of a sort to require blood-turning. What's the complaint? The wrong kind for this, I'll be bound."

"My arm." She reluctantly showed the withered skin.

"Ah! 'tis all a-scram!" said the hangman, examining it.

"Yes," said she.

"Well," he continued, with interest, "this *is* the class o' subject, I'm bound to admit! I like the look of the place; it is truly as suitable for the cure as any I ever saw. 'Twas a knowing man that sent 'ee, whoever he was."

"You can contrive for me all that's necessary?" she said, breathlessly.

"You should really have gone to the governor of the jail, and your doctor with 'ee, and given your name and address—that's how it used to be done, if I recollect. Still, perhaps I can manage it for a trifling fee."

"Oh, thank you! I would rather do it this way, as I should like it kept private."

"Lover not to know, eh?"

"No—husband."

"Aha! Very well. I'll get 'ee a touch of the corpse."

"Where is it now?" she said, shuddering.

"It?—*he*, you mean; he's living yet. Just inside that little small winder up there in the glum." He signified the jail on the cliff above.

She thought of her husband and her friends. "Yes, of course," she said; "and how am I to proceed?"

He took her to the door. "Now, do you be waiting at the little wicket in the wall, that you'll find up there in the lane, not later than one o'clock. I will open it from the inside, as I sh'n't come home to dinner till he's cut down. Good-night. Be punctual; and if you don't want anybody to know 'ee, wear a veil. Ah, once I had such a daughter as you!"

She went away, and climbed the path above, to assure herself that she would be able to find the wicket next day. Its outline was soon visible to her—a narrow opening in the outer wall of the prison precincts. The steep was so great that, having reached the wicket, she stopped a moment to breathe; and looking back upon the water-side cot, saw the hangman again ascending his out-door staircase. He entered the loft, or chamber, to which it led, and in a few minutes extinguished his light.

The town clock struck ten, and she returned to the White Hart as she had come.

IX

A RECOUNTER

It was one o'clock on Saturday. Gertrude Lodge, having been admitted to the jail as above described, was sitting in a waiting-room within the second gate, which stood under a classic archway of ashler, then comparatively modern, and bearing the inscription, "COUNTY JAIL: 1793". This had been the facade she saw from the heath the day before. Near at hand was a passage to the roof on which the gallows stood.

The town was thronged, and the market suspended; but Gertrude had seen scarcely a soul. Having kept her room till the hour of the appointment, she had proceeded to the spot by a way which avoided the open space below the cliff where the spectators had gathered; but she could, even now, hear the multitudinous babble of their voices, out of which rose at intervals the hoarse croak of a single voice, uttering the words, "Last dying speech and confession!" There had been no reprieve, and the execution was over; but the crowd still waited to see the body taken down.

Soon the persistent girl heard a trampling overhead, then a hand beckoned to her, and, following directions, she went out and crossed the inner paved court beyond the gate-house, her knees trembling so that she could scarcely walk. One of her arms was out of its sleeve, and only covered by her shawl.

On the spot to which she had now arrived were two trestles, and before she could think of their purpose she heard heavy feet descending stairs somewhere at her back. Turn her head she would not, or could not, and, rigid in this position, she was conscious of a rough coffin passing her shoulder, borne by four men. It was open, and in it lay the body of a young man, wearing the smock-frock of a rustic, and fustian breeches. It had been thrown into the coffin so hastily that the skirt of the smock-frock was hanging over. The burden was temporarily deposited on the trestles.

By this time the young woman's state was such that a gray mist seemed to float before her eyes, on account of which, and the veil she wore, she could scarcely discern anything; it was as though she had died but was held up by a sort of galvanism.

"Now," said a voice close at hand, and she was just conscious that it had been addressed to her.

By a last strenuous effort she advanced, at the same time hearing persons approaching behind her. She bared her poor cursed arm; and Davies, uncovering the dead man's face, took her hand, and held it so that the arm lay across the neck of the corpse, upon a line the color of an unripe blackberry which surrounded it.

Gertrude shrieked; "the turn o' the blood," predicted by the conjurer, had taken place. But at that moment a second shriek rent the air of the enclosure; it was not Gertrude's, and its effect upon her was to make her start round.

Immediately behind her stood Rhoda Brook, her face drawn, and her eyes red with weeping. Behind Rhoda stood her own husband; his countenance lined, his eyes dim, but without a tear.

"D—n you! what are you doing here?" he said, hoarsely.

"Hussy—to come between us and our child now!" cried Rhoda. "This is the meaning of what Satan showed me in the vision! You are like her at last!" And clutching the bare arm of the younger woman, she pulled her unresistingly back against the wall. Immediately Brook had loosened her hold the fragile young Gertrude slid down against the feet of her husband. When he lifted her up she was unconscious.

The mere sight of the twain had been enough to suggest to her that the dead young man was Rhoda's son. At that time the relatives of an executed convict had the privilege of claiming the body for burial, if they chose to do so; and it was for this purpose that Lodge was awaiting the inquest with Rhoda. He had been summoned by her as soon as the young man was taken in the crime, and at different times since; and he had attended in court during the trial. This was the "holiday" he had been indulging in of late. The two wretched parents had wished to avoid exposure; and hence had come themselves for the body, a wagon and a sheet for its conveyance and covering being in waiting outside.

Gertrude's case was so serious that it was deemed advisable to call to her the surgeon who was at hand. She was taken out of the jail into the town; but she never reached home alive. Her delicate vitality, sapped perhaps by the paralyzed arm, collapsed under the double shock that followed the severe strain, physical and mental, to which she had subjected herself during the previous twenty-four hours. Her blood had been "turned" indeed—too far. Her death took place in the town three days after.

Her husband was never seen in Casterbridge again; once only in the old market-place at Anglebury, which he had so much frequented, and very seldom in public anywhere. Burdened at first with moodiness and remorse, he eventually changed for the better, and appeared as a chastened and thoughtful man. Soon after attending the funeral of his poor young wife, he took steps towards giving up the farms in Holmstoke and the adjoining parish, and, having sold every head of his stock, he went away to Port-Bredy, at the other end of the county, living there in solitary lodgings till his death, two years later, of a painless decline. It was then found that he had bequeathed the whole of his not inconsiderable property to a reformatory for boys, subject to the payment of a small annuity to Rhoda Brook, if she could be found to claim it.

For some time she could not be found; but eventually she reappeared in her old parish—absolutely refusing, however, to have anything to do with the provision made for her. Her monotonous milking at the dairy was resumed, and followed for many long years, till her form became bent, and her once abundant dark hair white and worn away at the forehead—perhaps by long pressure against the cows. Here, sometimes, those who knew her experiences would stand and observe her, and wonder what sombre thoughts were beating inside that impassive, wrinkled brow, to the rhythm of the alternating milk-streams.

INTERNATIONAL : POCKET : LIBRARY

OTHER TITLES IN PREPARATION

INTERNATIONAL : POCKET : LIBRARY

OTHER TITLES IN PREPARATION